CASE OF THE MISSING TEETH

Written and Illustrated by Frank and Carol Hill

MODERN PUBLISHING
A Division of Unisystems, Inc.
New York, New York 10022

Sam Clam was good at finding things because his eyes were close to the ground.

Arnie Oyster lost his pearl, Tina Tuna lost her tricycle, Eli Electric Eel lost his battery and Sam found them all.

One day, Sam's old friend, Gummer Shark, arrived and told this story:

"I used to eat jellyfish jam on my kelp sandwiches but I didn't brush or floss my teeth very often."

"One morning when I woke up, my teeth were gone! I bought new ones but they were too loose."

"At my birthday party I made a wish and blew my teeth out instead of the candles. The current quickly carried them away."

"Let's see if we can find them," said Sam.

"Hi Bennie," said Sam. "We're looking for Gummer's teeth. Have you seen them?"

"Yes," said Bennie.

"Where are they?" asked Sam.

"They went thattaway," Bennie pointed. Sam and Gummer swam off.

They met Eli Electric Eel.
"Have you seen Gummer's teeth?"
Sam asked.
"I sure did! They nipped me on the nose and chomped off into the kelp forest," said Eli.

At the edge of the kelp forest, Sam and Gummer found a path. They followed the path deep into the forest.

"Look, Gummer, there they are!" said Sam.

Gummer tried to pick up the teeth.
"No! Go away!" squeaked a little voice from inside the teeth. "This is my house. You can't have it!"

"It's Kermit Hermit Crab!" said Gummer.
"We'll just have to find Kermit a new house,"
said Sam.

And so they did. Bennie sold them just the right thing.

An old, comfortable shoe for a new, cozy house. Kermit was happy and Gummer could smile once again.